Queen Clarion's Secret

Queen Clarion's Secret

WRITTEN BY
KIMBERLY MORRIS

ILLUSTRATED BY
DENISE SHIMABUKURO, ADRIENNE BROWN,
CHARLES PICKENS & ANDREW PHILLIPSON

A STEPPING STONE BOOK™
RANDOM HOUSE 🏠 NEW YORK

Library of Congress Cataloging-in-Publication Data

Morris, Kimberly.

Queen Clarion's secret / written by Kimberly Morris ; illustrated by
Denise Shimabukuro, Adrienne Brown, Charles Pickens
& Andrew Phillipson.

p. cm.

"A Stepping Stone book."

Summary: Fairies Beck, Prilla, and Lily investigate the disappearance of
Queen Clarion, the ruler of Pixie Hollow.

ISBN 978-0-7364-2547-6 (pbk.)

[1. Fairies—Fiction. 2. Kings, queens, rulers, etc.—Fiction.
3. Adventure and adventurers—Fiction.] I. Shimabukuro, Denise, ill.
II. Brown, Adrienne, ill. III. Pickens, Charles, ill.
IV. Phillipson, Andrew, ill. V. Title.

PZ7.M7881635Qu 2009

[Fic]—dc22   2008015686

www.randomhouse.com/kids

Printed in the United States of America

10 9 8 7 6 5 4 3 2 1

All About Fairies

IF YOU HEAD toward the second star on your right and fly straight on till morning, you'll come to Never Land, a magical island where mermaids play and children never grow up.

When you arrive, you might hear something like the tinkling of little bells. Follow that sound and you'll find Pixie Hollow, the secret heart of Never Land.

A great old maple tree grows in Pixie Hollow, and in it live hundreds of fairies and sparrow men. Some of them can do water magic, others can fly like the wind, and still others can speak to animals. You see, Pixie Hollow is the Never fairies' kingdom, and each fairy who lives there has a special, extraordinary talent.

Not far from the Home Tree, nestled in the branches of a hawthorn, is Mother Dove, the most magical creature of all. She sits on her egg, watching over the fairies, who in turn watch over her. For as long as Mother Dove's egg stays well and whole, no one in Never Land will ever grow old.

Once, Mother Dove's egg *was* broken. But we are not telling the story of the egg here. Now it is time for Queen Clarion's tale. . . .

Queen
Clarion's
Secret

"Look out, Prilla! Wheeeee!" Fira, a light-talent fairy, called. She whizzed past Prilla and accidentally clipped her wing. It sent Prilla into a spin. Prilla cartwheeled through the air and laughed with joy.

It was a sunny, windy day in Pixie Hollow. Unruly breezes had started up that morning, eager to tease and play. "I'm having a hard time steering in this wind!" Fira cried as a gust blew her away. "So I'm not even trying anymore."

Prilla righted herself by catching a branch. She looked up. The weather-talent fairies flew their weather kites high overhead. The kites were made of leaves woven together and covered with a thick layer of mica paint. The mica made the huge leaf kites look like glittering diamonds in the sky. Prilla loved watching them climb and dive.

Every once in a while, one of the kites escaped and careened through the sky. It darted, dashed, and swooped before finally coming to rest, caught in the branches of a tree. Other wayward kites flew up, up, and away—never to be seen again.

Prilla struggled to fly against the wind. She flapped her wings as hard as she could. But the bouncy gusts seemed to lift her up, push her back, and thrust her forward, all at the same time.

Prilla decided to stop trying. It was wearing her out. Why not just let the breeze take her for a ride, as it had with Fira? Prilla put one hand on top of her acorn hat to keep it from blowing off, and opened her wings. She coasted along a few feet above the ground.

"Coming through!" she heard a sparrow man say as he tumbled past her—backward. The wind had captured him like a kite.

The breeze changed direction and created a little funnel. Prilla and the sparrow man blew around each other in a circle. The sparrow man grinned.

"I'm trying to get to the fairy-dust mill," he said. "But I'm not having much luck. It's too hard to fly today. I think I'll walk instead."

Usually, fairies didn't walk if they could fly. But there were lots of fairies on the ground today.

The sparrow man folded his wings behind him and crossed his arms over his chest. He slid gracefully to the ground, then hiked off.

"Good luck!" Prilla cried after him.

Prilla turned a few backward somersaults above the ground. The added boost from the wind sent her spinning again.

She caught a branch and brought herself to a stop. *Maybe I could ride the breezes on my stomach*, she thought. She turned over and discovered that she could. She bounced through the air with her chin resting on her folded arms.

Prilla watched the ground below with interest. She saw three baking-talent fairies hurrying toward the Home

Tree kitchen to start the pastries for afternoon tea. She also saw Bess, an art-talent fairy. Bess was struggling to carry a large painting toward her studio. The painting acted like a sail in the breeze. Bess went flying off in the opposite direction, giggling.

Then Prilla saw Queen Clarion walking briskly toward Lily's garden. Prilla loved watching Queen Clarion. She was so beautiful and graceful—and just a bit mysterious.

What is it like to be a queen? Prilla wondered. *Is it hard or easy? What does the queen think about as she goes around on her daily business?*

As Prilla watched, Queen Clarion paused outside the low fence that circled

Lily's garden. The queen looked left and right. She glanced back over her shoulder. Then, as quick as lightning, Queen Clarion reached over the fence and snapped something from a bush. She thrust the object into her pocket. Lowering her head against the breeze, she walked away.

Prilla looked for the queen's attendants. The queen never went anywhere without at least two. Today, though, Queen Clarion seemed to be alone.

Maybe her attendants stayed indoors because of the wind, Prilla thought.

Prilla decided that she would ask the queen if she wanted company. She blushed happily at the idea of walking side by side with Queen Clarion.

What an honor that would be!

But just as Prilla was about to land, a shadow crossed the ground in front of her. She looked up and her eyes widened. A huge bird was soaring across the sky. It was unlike any bird Prilla had ever seen. The bird was as colorful as a parrot, but it was much longer. Its wingspan was as wide as an eagle's.

The bird traveled so fast that it left a multicolored streak in the sky behind it. Prilla felt a shiver of fear. A bird so big and fast could be dangerous to fairies. She would have to warn the queen.

But when she looked back, Queen Clarion was gone.

PRILLA LOOKED IN every direction. She scanned the ground and the air. Queen Clarion was nowhere to be seen.

How could Queen Clarion have disappeared so fast? Prilla wondered. But before she could think another thing about it, a breeze at her back turned her over and over like a bottle in the surf.

She tumbled through the air toward the kite-flying field. There, weather-talent fairies struggled with the weather kites.

Some of the kites were taller than five fairies and wider than six sparrow men. It took whole teams of fairies to control them. To Prilla, it looked like hard work, but the weather fairies enjoyed it.

Prilla folded her wings behind her, crossed her arms over her chest, and slid to the ground beside a row of fairies wrestling with a kite. She landed behind the last sparrow man. They needed help. She grabbed the rope with both hands and felt the fierce pull of the kite.

"Have you seen Queen Clarion?"

Prilla shouted to the sparrow man. Her voice could barely be heard over the whipping, snapping, and rushing sound of the kites.

The sparrow man shook his head. "Not today," he shouted back. "We've had our hands too full to notice anything or anybody." He smiled. "Wonderful, isn't it? This is the windiest day we've had in years. It's a day for the record books."

At the far end of the field, a group of weather fairies charted the direction and speed of the winds. They made careful notes in their leaf-page notebooks.

The sparrow man continued, "Down here, the breeze blows in all directions. It creates crosswinds and drafts." He jutted

his chin upward, drawing Prilla's attention to a high-flying kite straining against its line. "But when you get higher up you can see the wind is blowing south. That's unusual for this time of year."

They heard a loud whoop followed by laughter. On the other side of the field, one of the kites went barreling across the sky with three fairies hanging on to its tail.

It looked like wonderful fun to Prilla. Everybody else seemed to think so, too. Fairies came running from all directions to line up for a ride on a kite tail.

Prilla longed to ride a kite tail, too. But she was too curious about the queen to stick around. So she wished the weather-talent fairies luck, let go of the line, and allowed the breeze to tumble her along.

Within moments, she found herself at the Home Tree. Prilla looked down and saw that she was right over Queen Clarion's apartments. Maybe the wind had blown the queen back to the Home Tree, too!

Inside the queen's chambers, Prilla found Queen Clarion's attendants. Cinda and Rhia were tying dust covers across chairs. Lisel and Grace struggled to close the curtains. The curtains snapped loudly in the wind. "Is the queen here?" Prilla shouted.

At last, Lisel pulled the curtains shut. "Are you here for an appointment?"

she asked, while Grace wrestled with the ties. Without waiting for an answer, Lisel hurried to a large book on the desk. "I can't imagine where the queen is," she muttered. "She missed two appointments this morning. She must have forgotten."

Grace finished tying the curtains and turned to Prilla. "Sometimes we get so busy keeping track of the queen's schedule," she said with a laugh, "we forget to keep track of the queen!"

Should I tell Lisel and Grace that I saw the queen by Lily's garden? Prilla wondered. Then she remembered the way Queen Clarion had glanced over her shoulder. *Maybe she didn't want to be kept track of,* Prilla thought. Was it possible that the queen was off on some secret business that she didn't want her attendants to know about?

"That's okay," Prilla said quickly. "I didn't really have an appointment. I just . . . umm . . . thought I'd stop by. It's not important."

Prilla hurried away before anyone could ask her more questions. Whatever the queen was doing, she would surely be back in time for tea.

But at teatime, Queen Clarion was still nowhere to be seen. The tearoom was full of chattering fairies enjoying orange-peel cookies and lots of other goodies. Prilla felt too uneasy to enjoy anything.

She sipped her tea. But her throat was so tight it was hard to make the tea go down. *A queen shouldn't go around alone,* Prilla thought. *Anything could happen. She could be attacked by a hawk or a pirate or a wasp. Or . . . or she could even die of disbelief.*

When a child anywhere in the world stopped believing in fairies, a fairy faded away. Disbelief was the worst thing that could happen to a fairy. But Prilla could save a fairy from disbelief. It was her special talent. In the blink of an eye, Prilla would travel to the mainland and ask children to clap to show that they believed. If enough children clapped, they could save a fairy's life.

Prilla's breath caught in her chest.

Was it possible that the queen needed saving?

Stop being silly, Prilla told herself. Queen Clarion was very sensible. She took an interest in every part of fairy life. She had probably gone to check on the dairy-mouse barn or the fairy-dust mill. Flying against the wind, she could easily fall behind schedule.

Still, Prilla couldn't help worrying. The sooner she found Queen Clarion, the sooner she could relax.

Prilla pushed what was left of her orange-peel cookie away. She would go to the dairy-mouse barn and the fairy-dust mill herself. She would keep looking all over Pixie Hollow until she found the queen.

When Prilla got to the mill, she found that the dust-talent fairies weren't as happy about the visiting breezes as the rest of Pixie Hollow. Tarps woven out of leaves and pounded bark covered every bin and barrel of fairy dust.

The mill was a flurry of activity. The dust-talent fairies would get one batch of fairy dust covered with a tarp. Then the breeze would come along and whiffle it. Clouds of fairy dust flew everywhere.

Terence, a fairy-dust-talent sparrow man, hurried from bin to barrel. Prilla hated to bother him, but she tugged on the sleeve of his tunic anyway.

"Terence, have you seen Queen Clarion?" she asked.

Terence used a rock to hold a tarp down on top of a barrel. "No," he said. "At least, I don't think I have. I've been so busy with the mill that I don't know who I have seen. Or who I haven't."

A gust of wind blew a barrel of dust over. The entire group of dust-talent fairies hurried to set it upright. They were determined to keep the dust from blowing away. Terence turned and went back to his work.

Prilla left the fairy-dust mill and hiked to the crown-repair workshop, the kitchen, and even Tinker Bell's pots-and-pans-repair workshop. But everyone was busy, and no one had seen the queen.

Prilla sighed heavily. She spread her wings and let the breeze carry her along backward in the direction of the dairy-mouse barn.

She had almost reached it when, suddenly, she bumped into something in midair.

And the something went, "*Oomph!*"

3

PRILLA TURNED HER head and saw that the "something" was Lily, who was a garden-talent fairy.

Lily giggled. "Oops! I was surfing the breeze and wasn't paying a bit of attention."

The two fairies dropped to the ground to get out of the wind. Lily glanced at Prilla's worried face. "What's the matter, Prilla? Did I hurt you?"

Prilla shook her head. "No. I'm not hurt," she said.

"Is something wrong?" Lily asked.

Prilla pressed her lips together. She didn't want to start a panic, but she needed to talk to someone. "Well, I can't find the queen anywhere!"

Lily smiled. "Queens don't just disappear," she said. "I'll help you find her. Where was the last place you saw her?"

"Your garden," Prilla answered.

"My garden!" Lily echoed. "The queen was in my garden?" She sounded pleased and concerned at the same time. "I hope it was tidy. Come on, Prilla. Let's go see."

At the garden, Lily let out a sigh of relief. "Everything looks nice. I'm glad the wind didn't blow over any of my flowers. Wait!" Lily said suddenly. "Look over there. What is that?"

Prilla's eyes followed the direction of Lily's pointing finger. She gasped. A scrap of pink lace fluttered from a thorny rosebush.

They hurried to the rosebush. Prilla pulled the lace off the thorn. It looked like a piece of the queen's dress!

She turned to show it to Lily, but Lily was staring at a pink rose. She drew in her breath. "Oh, no!" Lily whispered. "I can't believe it."

"What? What happened?" Prilla asked.

"This is a Fairy Pink rosebush," Lily explained. "It's the only one in Pixie Hollow. One Fairy Pink rose grows each year. In the middle of the rose is a heart seed. The rose bloomed this morning. But look! The heart seed is gone!"

"What is a heart seed?" Prilla asked.

"It's the sweetest and most delicious

tidbit in all of Never Land," answered Lily.

"I saw the queen pluck something earlier," Prilla said. "Maybe it was the heart seed."

"That's impossible," Lily protested. "That seed is for Mother Dove. Queen Clarion would never take it. I always give it to Mother Dove myself. I was going to do it this afternoon."

"Maybe Queen Clarion took it to Mother Dove," Prilla suggested. "Come on! Let's go see Beck. She'll know if the queen is visiting Mother Dove."

Mother Dove's nest sat in the hawthorn tree near the fairy circle. Beck, the animal-talent fairy who took care of Mother Dove, was usually nearby.

The hawthorn tree wasn't far from Lily's garden. But the gusts and breezes made the short trip seem to take forever. The wind picked the fairies up, then put them down. It pushed them sideways, then blew them back to where they had started.

When they finally got to the hawthorn tree, they found Beck curled up on the ground between its roots. A tiny bird sat happily in her lap. Lily asked her if Queen Clarion was visiting Mother Dove.

Beck sent the bird on its way. "No. Queen Clarion isn't here," she told Lily. "She hasn't been here all day."

"Are you sure?" Lily asked.

"I'm sure," said Beck.

Prilla let out a little squeak of confusion. Lily pressed her hands against her face.

"What's wrong?" Beck asked.

Prilla described what she had seen that morning. Lily told her about the missing heart seed.

"What could it all mean?" Prilla asked.

"I think it means there's a mystery. And we need to find Queen Clarion to solve it," said Beck. "The last place you saw her was outside Lily's garden. So that's where we'll begin."

Beck started off—on foot—toward Lily's garden. Prilla and Lily followed.

After a short while, Lily said, "You know, I love to fly more than anything in the world. But it's nice to walk every now and then. I notice things I would never see otherwise."

"Like what?" Prilla asked. They were getting close to the garden now.

Lily pointed. "Like these footprints. You can barely see them, but they're there. Whoever made them was very light. Too light to flatten the blades of grass, but heavy enough to bend them."

Prilla got excited. "Do you think they're the queen's footprints?" she asked.

Lily bent down to examine the ground. "There's no way to be sure. But they go right up to the fence of my

garden. Then they go this way. And then . . ." Lily straightened up and met Prilla's gaze.

"What is it?" Prilla asked.

"The footprints. They just . . . stop."

4

"Do you think the fairy who made them flew from here?" Prilla asked. "Or maybe the wind blew her away."

"Maybe," said Beck. But she seemed to be thinking of something else. She dropped down and pressed her ear to the ground. "Yep! Just what I thought."

Prilla and Lily dropped down and

pressed their ears to the ground, too. "I don't hear anything," Prilla said.

"Me neither," Lily said.

"You don't hear all the chattering?" Beck asked. Her eyes were wide with surprise.

Prilla and Lily shook their heads.

"I guess you have to be an animal talent," Beck said. "We're above the tunnels. The animal talents built them so we could move around easily, but a lot of animals take shelter in them. From the sound of it, the critters down there are all excited about something."

Prilla bounced to her feet. "Maybe Queen Clarion decided to use the tunnels today to get around!"

"Or maybe she fell into one by

accident." Beck took a few steps and pointed to a hole in the ground. It was hidden by a big fern leaf. "She wouldn't be the first."

Prilla stood on the edge of the hole. She put her arms out and let herself teeter back and forth. She was eager to drop in and explore the mysterious tunnel. "So are we going down to look?"

"You bet!" Beck said.

Prilla didn't wait another moment. She jumped into the hole. But it was too narrow for her to fully spread her wings. She landed on the soft earth below with a *THUD!* Prilla rolled quickly aside. A second later—*THUMP!*—Lily came tumbling behind her.

Prilla stretched out a hand and

helped Lily to her feet. Next down was Beck. She landed gracefully. She'd had a lot of practice.

Prilla looked around. The tunnel was dark. The only light came through the hole above their heads and from their glows.

Prilla had never been underground before. It was a whole different world, strange and exciting at the same time.

Beck led the way, and Prilla and Lily followed her.

When Prilla's eyes grew used to the dim light, she was amazed to see that the tunnel wasn't really empty. Twisting roots and plant tendrils stuck out of the dirt. Between them, earthworms wriggled lazily. The packed earth walls

of the tunnel smelled damp and rich.

As the fairies walked, sleeping pill-bugs briefly uncurled to see who was passing by. Then they curled back up. A line of ants scurried up the path. Some stopped to curiously inspect the fairies. Others paid no attention at all.

Beck had said it was noisy, but to

Prilla's ears, the tunnel was eerily quiet. She saw the moving life all around her, but she couldn't hear the chatter of the worms and insects.

"This is spooky," Lily whispered.

Prilla nodded. They both huddled closer behind Beck.

A squeaking noise made them jump and press their backs against the wall of the tunnel. Beck laughed as five baby mice came running by. They sped past the fairies without so much as a how-de-do and vanished in the dark.

"I wonder where they're going in such a hurry?" Beck mused.

Lily said, "If Queen Clarion is down here and has the heart seed, they're running to find her. Animals love the scent and the taste of a heart seed. In fact," she added thoughtfully, "it could be dangerous to have a heart seed in your pocket. An animal might think that *you* are the tidbit that smells so delicious."

At that moment, the five baby mice came running back. This time they were going twice as fast. They practically ran over one another as they scrambled out of the tunnel.

"What is—" They turned a corner, and the words died on Beck's lips.

Prilla looked past her and saw why. There, straight ahead of them, was a snake. A *big* snake, sound asleep.

In the snake's narrow middle was a bulge. He had recently swallowed a large meal. Prilla's heart began to race, and

Lily's words echoed in her head: *It could be dangerous to have a heart seed in your pocket. An animal might think that you are the tidbit that smells so delicious.*

Prilla's eyes widened in horror. *Oh, no! Could that bulge be . . . Queen Clarion?*

5

"BECK," PRILLA WHISPERED, "I think he sees us."

The snake had opened one eye.

"Stay calm," Beck whispered. "Don't show any fear."

The snake lifted his head. He studied the three fairies.

Beck took a step back and made a

series of hissing snake sounds. The snake's head swayed as if he was listening. He hissed an answer.

"What's he saying?" Prilla whispered. "What's he saying? Did you ask him what he ate?" Prilla felt Beck's elbow dig into her side. "*Ouch!*"

"Shhh," Beck warned out of the side of her mouth.

Beck spoke to the snake again. Then she started to back away. Prilla and Lily had to back away, too.

"Ask him what he had for lunch," Lily whispered.

Beck looked back at Prilla and Lily. "Snakes are very polite," she said. "I can't just ask him flat out what he ate. That would be rude."

Prilla bit her lip. "Then how are we going to find out?"

"Let me talk to him," Beck said. "You two get ready to run in case he doesn't feel like chatting. Snakes can be moody."

Prilla watched Beck approach the snake again. Beck was so brave! Meanwhile, Prilla's heart was beating so loudly, she was surprised it didn't echo in the tunnel. The snake moved closer. His eyes glittered dangerously.

The snake's tongue flicked faster. The conversation seemed to take an awfully long time. The snake's face swayed in front of Beck. Prilla stared at his hinged jaw. She knew it could open like a door and swallow a fairy—or two or three—whole.

"Maybe we should run," Lily whispered in a trembling voice.

"No! Wait!" Prilla said, even though she was shaking from head to toe. "I think they're done. Here she comes."

Beck was backing toward them with great care. "Let's go," she whispered as she turned slowly. "We don't want to seem rude. Just walk calmly back the way we came."

Prilla forced herself to walk and not run. But she couldn't hold back her fear. She had to know. "Well? Did you find out what he ate?"

"He ate an egg," Beck whispered as they rounded a corner. As soon as they were out of the snake's sight, she added, "*Now* run!"

The hole was only a few feet away. The fairies shot out of the tunnel and into the sunlight.

"Thank goodness he didn't eat Queen Clarion," Prilla gasped. She turned a few cartwheels to show her relief.

"Yes. But listen to this," Beck said. "He told me that he was asleep in a tree earlier today. On a weather kite. And somebody tipped him off it. Whoever did it smelled delicious, he said."

"Queen Clarion!" Lily exclaimed. "It had to be. She smelled delicious because she had the heart seed."

"Maybe. Maybe not," replied Beck. "I'll bet all fairies smell delicious to a snake. Or it could have been a squirrel or a possum. But let's imagine it was Queen Clarion. *Why* would she tip the snake off a kite? She's usually very considerate."

"Because she wanted the kite," Lily guessed. "It would be too risky to ask him to move. He might eat her. So she had to tip him off the kite when he wasn't looking."

"But why would Queen Clarion want a kite?" Beck asked.

As if to answer the question, another gust of wind came racing around the bend. It lifted Prilla's hat off her head, and she scrambled after it.

"Maybe she wanted to go somewhere," suggested Prilla. "And she wanted to use wind to get there."

Lily nodded. "That's possible. Or maybe she was just trying to bring it back for the weather-talent fairies. If she got tangled up in it, the wind would have carried her off."

"Which way would she have gone?" Beck asked.

"I know how to find out," Prilla said with a grin. "Come on!"

6

"Isn't this fun!" Prilla cried as the kite flew higher.

Prilla, Lily, and Beck all sat on knots in the tail of the biggest weather kite in the field. Prilla sat on the topmost knot. Beck sat on the knot in the middle. And Lily sat on the knot at the bottom.

Far below them, on the ground, twenty strong fairies and sparrow men fought to hold on to the kite. The kite strained against the line.

Prilla was dizzy with excitement. She had never been so high up! She could see shores, horizons, and the mysterious lands all around Never Land.

Directly south, right in the path of the wind, was a dense forest. The trees were so tall that their tops were hidden in the clouds.

"Look at those trees!" Prilla cried. She had to shout to be heard over the roaring of the wind and the snapping of the kite.

"That's the High Tree Forest," Lily called up to the others.

Prilla leaned down to shout at Lily. "What's there? I mean, besides the trees?"

"Animals and birds," Beck answered for her. "Lots of them."

"Do you think . . . ?" The rest of Lily's question was carried away by the wind.

But Prilla guessed what Lily was thinking, and she nodded. "If Queen Clarion blew away on a kite, that's where she might land—or crash."

"We've got to go look for her!" Lily cried.

"But how will we get there?" Beck asked. "We don't have nearly enough fairy dust to fly that far. And we'd need twice as much dust with this wind."

Lily hesitated for a second. Then she reached into the pocket of her tunic and pulled out a pair of gardening shears. With one snip, she cut the thick rope that linked them to the ground.

"Aiiiiiiiieee!" Prilla shouted.

The moment the kite was free, it soared into the air. It climbed higher and higher, and flew faster and faster. Wind rushed past Prilla's ears. It made them so cold, she felt as if they might freeze. She was thrilled and terrified at the same time.

All she could do was hold tight to the tail. She wanted to close her eyes. But as scared as she was, she didn't want to miss one moment of the amazing ride.

The world seemed to twist and turn. Below them, mile after mile of Never Land raced by as they soared across the sky.

The High Tree Forest was coming closer. Prilla could see the thick trees. Their branches and leaves spread out to make a dense canopy of green. The forest was directly in their path.

"How are we going to stop?" she yelled.

"We'll make a soft landing in the leaves," Lily shouted. "Don't wor—"

Before the words *don't worry* were out of Lily's mouth, her eyes filled with alarm. Two birds were barreling toward them. It was clear they thought the kite should get out of *their* path and not the other way around. They didn't even slow down.

The birds flew through the kite,

tearing two large holes in it. The kite
began to fall. It faltered as it dropped.
The tattered edges of the holes rattled
and snapped.

When the kite got close to the
ground, the fairies let go of the tail and
spread their wings. They landed right at
the edge of the High Tree Forest.

"Now what?" Prilla asked the other two. She wasn't feeling nearly as brave now as when they started their search.

"Now we find the queen," Beck answered.

Lily led the way into the forest. The tree trunks were gigantic. Even the smallest trunk was wider than the Home Tree.

Lily hurried from one plant to another. "Look at this color!" she cried. "Look at this shape!"

Prilla bounced along behind Lily. The flowers *were* very pretty here! But just then, Beck tilted her head.

"Shhh," she whispered.

Prilla's heart began to beat faster. "What do you hear?" she asked.

"The usual. Foxes, raccoons, hedge-hogs, bugs, a few snakes. But there's something else, too. Some creature is making a sound that I've never heard before. It sounds like some kind of bird."

Lily's smile faded. "Then we need to find Queen Clarion soon. If she has that seed in her pocket, birds are especially dangerous."

Beck looked up. "If Queen Clarion was on a kite, she probably crashed into the top of one of these trees. Maybe we should fly to the top of the tallest tree. That way, we'll see the whole forest. We'll spot that shiny kite in no time at all."

The fairies took a few steps deeper

into the forest. They left the sun behind and entered into the damp gloom.

Colorful mushrooms crept up the sides of tree trunks. The fairies tilted their heads back and stared up at the soaring trees. The treetops all came together overhead in a thick umbrella of branches and leaves.

"But which tree is the tallest?" Prilla asked. "They all look tall to me." The breeze kicked up and ruffled her curls. They tickled her forehead. "We'd have to fly as high as the clouds to find out."

Prilla had never flown that high before. She wasn't even sure she could. What if her wings gave out midway?

"I have an idea!" Lily pointed to the trunk of a tree. A thick climbing vine

wound its way all around the tree and circled upward. Lily stepped onto the vine and began to walk around the tree trunk.

"It's just like a circular staircase," she said with a delighted laugh. "We can climb up to the treetops on this. From there we'll figure out which tree is the tallest. Easy!" Lily dusted her hands together as if their task were already done.

7

PRILLA FELT AS if she had followed Beck
for miles. Up and around. Up and
around. Up and around. The climb was
long, and not at all easy.

About halfway up, Prilla and Beck
came to a big knothole. "Let's wait here
for Lily," Prilla suggested. Lily had fallen
behind because she kept stopping to
look at plants.

Prilla sat on the edge of the knot-hole with her back to the opening. It felt good to rest a little.

But suddenly, a tingle went down her spine. *Something was watching her!*

Prilla jumped up and whirled around. Two beady red eyes stared out from inside the dark opening.

"Beck! Look at that!" she cried. "Something is in there!"

Beck peeked into the knothole. After a moment, she called back, "It's just a tree frog! She's coming out to say hello."

POP . . . POP . . . POP . . . POP!

The tree frog's skinny arms and legs stretched out when she walked. With each step along the branch, her fingers and toes made odd popping sounds.

"What's that noise?" Prilla asked.

"It's the sticky pads on her fingers and toes," Beck answered. "That's how she hangs on to the tree."

The frog was green with bright red eyes. She stopped in a thatch of leaves a few inches away from the fairies. Then she peeped to Beck in Frog.

"She wants to know who we are," Beck said to Prilla. "I'll tell her we're fairies from Pixie Hollow." Beck peeped back at the frog. Then she squatted down and stuck her leg out at an angle.

"Tree frogs speak in different ways from other frogs," she told Prilla. "Body language means a lot to them."

POP . . . POP . . . POP . . . POP!

The frog took a few steps away. Then she closed her eyes.

"I guess she doesn't know what a fairy from Pixie Hollow is," Beck said.

"Tell her we've lost our queen and we're here to find her," Prilla urged. "Ask her if she's seen another fairy creature like us."

"I'll tell her we're just visiting and don't mean any harm." Beck hopped along the branch like a frog. She flicked a finger against her cheek to make *POP . . . POP . . . POP . . . POP!* sounds.

The frog came closer to the fairies again. She hung upside down, ready to leap away at the first sign of trouble.

Beck hooked one of her own legs

over a branch and hung down like the frog. She blinked her eyes and moved her elbows around as she spoke in Frog. Every now and then, she flipped her finger against her cheek to make a *POP . . . POP!* noise.

The frog puffed up her neck.

Beck held her breath until her face turned red.

The frog quivered, as if she was very excited. She changed her position on the branch.

Prilla watched Beck stick out her leg and pull it back in several times. When she wasn't moving her arms or swaying, she was puffing her cheeks in and out.

Beck and the frog chatted in Frog for a long time.

Zzzzzzz! A gnat flew by. In an instant, the frog's tongue snaked out. She snatched the gnat out of the air less than a centimeter from Prilla's ear.

The frog hardly seemed to notice what she had done. She kept on talking to Beck, with just a break to swallow her snack.

Prilla watched with growing impatience. Goodness! Animals sure did seem to be long-winded.

Finally, Beck dropped from the branch overhead and hovered next to Prilla. "It's a good thing frogs like to gossip. She told me all about how the owl in the next tree isn't speaking to the weasel family that lives in the trunk. She also told me that everybody today is chattering about a mysterious stranger in the forest."

"A mysterious stranger! It must be Queen Clarion!" Prilla cried. "Where is she?"

"In the canopy," Beck answered. "That's all she knows. I also asked her which tree in the forest is the tallest. She said she doesn't get out much during the day. But if we want to wait until nighttime, she can take us right to it."

A shiver went through Prilla's wings. *Nighttime!* She couldn't imagine anything scarier than being in this forest at night.

Beck put a hand on Prilla's arm. "Don't worry," she said. "I told her we had to be home by dark."

Prilla looked at the sky. "But *can* we get home by dark?" The day was quickly drawing to a close.

"We can if we find Queen Clarion soon. But . . ." Beck frowned suddenly. "Where is Lily? She should have caught up by now."

"You're right." Prilla gulped. They

hadn't seen Lily in ages. Something must be wrong!

Prilla had learned a lot of things living in the Home Tree. One of them was the fastest way down a circular staircase. She dropped to her backside and began sliding down the vine.

"Lily!" she shouted. "Lily, where are you?"

Beck came behind her. "Lily!" she yelled. "Lily, we're coming!"

8

WHERE WAS LILY? Where? At every knothole, Prilla and Beck screeched to a stop and stuck their heads inside. They startled a family of squirrels, a sleeping owl, and a colony of spiders. But they saw no sign of Lily.

Then they heard a distant cry. "Help! Help!"

"Come on, let's fly!" Beck told Prilla. The two fairies left the vine and flew around the tree until they finally saw Lily. She was pinned under a fallen branch. The twigs made a little cage that held her fast.

Prilla and Beck flew to the branch and tried to move it. It was too heavy.

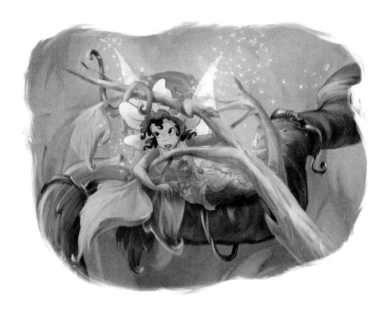

They tried to snap the twigs. Even the smallest one was too thick.

"What happened?" Beck asked. "Are you hurt?"

"I'm fine. But I'm stuck," answered Lily. "I was watching the squirrels in this tree playing. When they jumped from one branch to the other, this branch broke off and fell on me."

"We'll have to use our fairy dust to help us move it," Beck said.

"No, we'll need every speck of dust we have to get home," Lily protested.

Fairies needed dust to fly and do magic. But Beck, Prilla, and Lily only had the dust on their wings. They'd left Pixie Hollow in such a hurry that they hadn't thought to bring extra fairy dust.

"There has to be a better way," Lily said.

Suddenly, a loud noise startled them all. *Ratatatatata ratatatatata ratatatatata!*

"It's a woodpecker!" Beck cried. "I'll go get him. He can break up this branch in seconds."

"Wait!" Prilla stopped her. "There are lots of animals in this tree. What if one of them tries to get Lily? She can't fly away. *You* might be able to talk an animal out of it. But *I* couldn't."

"What else can we do?" Beck asked.

"I can't *talk* to the woodpecker. But maybe I could lead him here and *you* could talk to him," Prilla said.

"I have an idea," Beck said. "Lily, can you reach your shears?"

"Yes. Here." Lily gave Beck the shears.

"Listen to this pattern," Beck said to Prilla. "It's Woodpecker for *Help! Follow me!*" Beck tapped the shears on the tree.

Beck handed Prilla the shears. "Now you try it."

Prilla banged the shears on the bark.

Beck grinned. "Perfect! Now go find the woodpecker and bring him back. You may have a hard time getting his attention, though. Woodpeckers are not good listeners. Their heads are harder than tree trunks."

"I'll find a way," Prilla promised.

She took off into the forest, trying to follow the woodpecker's sound. It was hard to figure out where it was coming from because of the forest echo.

At last, Prilla spotted the woodpecker's red head. He held on to the side of a tree with his toes and pecked furiously against the trunk. *Ratatatatata ratatatatata ratatatatata ratatatatata!*

Prilla fluttered around him and waved her arms, trying to attract his attention. But the woodpecker never missed a beat. He didn't even seem to know that she was there. *Ratatatatata ratatatatata ratatatatata ratatatatata!*

Finally, Prilla plucked a small pinecone from a branch and threw it as hard as she could. The pinecone smacked the woodpecker on the back of his hard head.

The woodpecker whipped around to see who, or what, had just hit him.

When he saw Prilla, he cocked his head to one side and stared at her with a hurt expression. His face seemed to say, *Why did you hit me? What did I ever do to you?*

Prilla took the shears and tapped them on the tree trunk exactly the way Beck had shown her.

The woodpecker cocked his head the other way in surprise.

Prilla tapped the shears again and repeated her call for help. She hoped she was tapping the right thing. What if she got it wrong? Maybe she was tapping *Eat me* instead of *Follow me!*

Then the woodpecker spread his wings. She had given him the right message!

But when Prilla turned to go, she

paused. Her eyes darted from one large tree trunk to another. They all looked the same.

Oh, no! She couldn't remember which tree Lily and Beck were in!

9

THE WOODPECKER LOOKED at Prilla. Prilla looked at the trees. They all seemed exactly alike!

How does Lily tell one silly plant from another? Prilla wondered.

She gave the woodpecker a weak smile. He cocked his head to the side. Prilla hovered in the air, then started flying toward one tree. The woodpecker was right behind her. She flew more and more slowly.

Then Prilla heard a far-off sound. *Ratatatatata ratatatatata ratatatatata ratatatatata!*

Prilla recognized the sound and the message. It was Beck. She was tapping out her own cry for help. If Prilla could hear it, that meant they were close.

The woodpecker heard it, too. He peeled off and zoomed away toward the sound.

This time, Prilla followed *him*. It was hard to keep up, but the patch of red on his head made him easy to spot. The woodpecker reached the tree before Prilla.

By the time she got there, Beck was explaining the situation. The woodpecker went to work. Within moments, the branch was in splinters and Lily was free.

"Good job!" Beck told Prilla.

"Come on," Lily urged. "We've got to get moving. The sun will be going down soon."

The woodpecker continued pecking along the branch where Lily had been trapped. He had lost interest in the fairies. Now he was busy looking for bugs.

"Should we ask him if he's seen the mysterious stranger?" Beck asked.

Prilla shook her head. "No. You probably would have to hit him on the head with a pinecone like I did. And this time, he might not be so nice about it."

They were getting close to the canopy. The day was almost over. The few remaining rays of sunlight that filtered down through the branches were shifting. Still, the fairies kept climbing.

Finally, they found themselves in a strange place. All around them was lush, thick plant life. It was greener and damper than any garden they had ever seen. Big, waxy leaves sprouted huge red and yellow flowers.

Lily sighed happily. "This is it," she told the others. "We're in the canopy. Isn't it wonderful?"

Prilla didn't think so. This place might seem wonderful to a garden-talent fairy, but to Prilla, it felt too crowded. The leaves, flowers, and vines grew so thick, they almost blocked out all the sunlight. She liked blue sky and open spaces better.

Beck seemed to feel the same way. "This is even worse than the forest floor," she protested. "It's like a jungle. We can't see a thing. How are we going to find the tallest tree?"

"Easy," Lily said. "Follow me." Lily ran through the wide tree branches. With grace and ease, she hopped from one leaf to the next. "Watch out," she said, pointing to a vine. "That one's poisonous."

Prilla followed her, trying not to slip. The air was cool. Moist bits of cloud trailed past her cheeks. Little by little, Lily's happiness rubbed off on Prilla. The forest canopy started to seem like an amazing place. It was so wild and untouched.

Finally, Lily came to a stop. She looked around, and then she spoke. "This is it. This is the tallest tree. If we can get to the top of this tree, we'll be able to see for miles. And we'll surely find Queen Clarion if she's here."

"How do you know it's the tallest tree?" Beck asked.

"Trust me," Lily said with a confident smile. She pointed to the strange plants that grew along the trunk of the tree and on its branches. "Look at that orchid. See how it holds up its head? See how that mushroom leans back and looks up? All the plants here stand straight and true—just like Queen Clarion's attendants. These plants know they're part of the tallest tree. And they're proud of that."

Prilla looked at the plants and chuckled. "Lily's right. They do remind me of Lisel, Grace, Cinda, and Rhia."

"I'm *sure* this is the tallest tree," Lily insisted. "Now let's go!"

Prilla opened her wings. Soon they were all flying straight up.

The winds were strong up here. The treetops swayed back and forth. Just as the fairies were reaching the very limits

of their strength, they saw her. *Queen Clarion!*

She sat on the uppermost branch of the tree. A large silver weather kite was wedged into the branches next to her.

Above her, gliding in a circle, was the huge bird that Prilla had seen that morning.

Beck let out an angry yell. Lily gasped.

Queen Clarion turned at the sound of their voices. When she saw them, her eyes lit up.

"What a surprise! How in the world did you get here?" she asked.

All the joy Prilla had felt in finding Queen Clarion had evaporated. Now she felt pure, sheer terror.

"Your Majesty!" Lily screamed. "Be careful. You are in grave danger."

"Because of this?" Queen Clarion opened her hand and held it out to show them what was in her palm—a small, perfectly formed heart-shaped seed. Its scent perfumed the air. The smell was so sweet, Prilla's head reeled.

The bird was right over Queen Clarion now. He opened his pointed beak.

"NO!" Prilla, Lily, and Beck all shouted. "*NO!*"

10

PRILLA WATCHED IN horror as the enormous bird bore down on the queen. But instead of scooping her up and carrying her away, he hovered for only a moment.

Gently, he took the heart seed from her palm.

The bird dipped his head, as if in

thanks. Then he beat his wings against the air and took to the sky. Soon he was gliding away on the same gusty winds that had carried them all to the High Tree Forest.

Prilla, Lily, and Beck hurried to Queen Clarion's side. They had to hold tight to the leaves and branches to keep from being blown away.

Queen Clarion invited them all to sit beside her. "I suppose you would like to know why I came here with Mother Dove's heart seed," she said.

It was late in the day, and the sun was just beginning to set. Pools of pink and orange streaked the sky. Prilla was happy just to sit and enjoy the lovely sound of Queen Clarion's voice.

"That was the Sky Bird," the queen explained. "He is Mother Dove's oldest and dearest friend. Long ago, before Mother Dove got her magic, they flew together in these skies."

Queen Clarion went on, "But now, because of her egg, Mother Dove is bound to the earth and to her nest. Because he is so large, the Sky Bird cannot land on the ground. If he did, he might never become airborne again. So he must always fly high and live among the cliffs, where the winds are constant and strong."

"But I saw him this morning," Prilla said. "Above Pixie Hollow."

Queen Clarion nodded. "Every few years, a strong wind blows over Never

Land. A wind strong enough to carry the Sky Bird close to Pixie Hollow. When that happens, the Sky Bird and Mother Dove trade greetings and gifts. Because Mother Dove can't fly, and the Sky Bird can't land, I am the go-between. Mother Dove sensed that the wind was coming, and she asked me to bring her gift to the Sky Bird."

"Did the Sky Bird have a gift for Mother Dove?" Lily asked.

Queen Clarion showed them a small fruit that shimmered like mother-of-pearl. She invited them each to touch it. The fruit was smooth as a plum and cold as an icicle.

"It's a fruit that grows only on the ice-cold windy cliffs of the Sky Bird's home," Queen Clarion explained.

"I don't understand," Beck said. "Why didn't Mother Dove tell us? We could have helped you."

Queen Clarion stood and unwound the kite tail from the branch. "Because fairies love to fly more than anything. Mother Dove knows it would be hard for them to believe that a bird who once soared could be happy anywhere but the sky. Mother Dove doesn't want you to worry that she's unhappy—because she's not."

The fairies were silent, thinking about Mother Dove and the Sky Bird.

"It's almost time for me to take Mother Dove her dinner," Beck said at last.

"We should be going now," the queen said, nodding. "The wind has shifted direction. With a little fairy dust, we'll be back in time for dinner."

Queen Clarion showered the kite with the twinkling fairy dust. The flickering mica on the kite began to glow.

"Everyone hang on," she told the others. Each fairy grabbed a knot on the tail.

Queen Clarion gave a yank and freed the kite from its wedge.

WHOOSH!

The powerful wind grabbed the kite as if it were being snatched up by a tornado.

Prilla hung on for dear life. But once again she wouldn't shut her eyes.

She didn't want to miss a single thing!

The fairy dust helped the kite chart its course back toward Pixie Hollow. Soon they were moving through the air in a smooth line. They passed through clouds made of sunset colors. Around them, the sky was stained orange, pink, and purple.

Prilla swayed on the kite tail. She felt like a queen herself—the queen of the world! There was no better way to fly than on a sparkly kite.

Prilla looked at the faces of her friends. Was Lily sad to be leaving the wondrous plants in the High Tree Forest? Maybe, but Prilla knew that she also missed her own garden back in Pixie Hollow. Lily would be glad to be home in time to water her plants before night.

Beck had a little smile on her face. Prilla guessed she was pleased that Mother Dove would get a gift that would make her so happy.

And the queen . . . ?

Well, it was hard to know what the queen was thinking.

Queens are not like the rest of us. They must be wise and gracious. They must be generous and kind. They must be brave, but also cautious. They must solve everyone's problems and keep everyone's secrets.

Most of all, they must keep their thoughts to themselves. So we cannot know what Queen Clarion was thinking.

Perhaps she was thinking it was a wonderful thing to be queen. Or perhaps not.

Only Queen Clarion knows.

Turn the page
for the first
chapter of the
next Disney Fairies
adventure,

Myka

Finds

Her

Way

MYKA WOKE WITH a start. She leaped from her bed and landed lightly on her toes. Some sort of noise had just echoed through Pixie Hollow. It could mean trouble. Fully alert, she darted to her bedroom window.

Myka's room was in the uppermost branch of the Home Tree. A knothole window stretched from floor to ceiling along an entire wall.

Myka slipped her sea-glass binoculars from the peg by her bed. Then she gazed out the window. Not one leaf rustled. Not one moth beat its wings.

But while she'd been sleeping, she *had* heard a noise. She was certain of it. The noise had made her toes tingle. But now . . . now . . . the air was still. In the darkness before sunrise, even the birds and crickets were silent.

Yet her instincts told her something was wrong.

Myka was a scouting-talent fairy. Her job was to warn other fairies of danger. She kept on guard for hawks and owls and other animals that preyed on fairies. She sniffed for out-of-control fires on the far side of Never Land. And she listened for angry wasps buzzing near Havendish Stream. All five of Myka's senses were razor-sharp.

And if a noise woke her in the middle of the night, she was ready to check it out. It was all part of being a scout.

Myka couldn't waste another minute. She reached for her quiver, which was filled with porcupine quill darts. Then she flew outside.

Darkness pressed in close. Myka felt as if she were the only fairy in the world. She circled the Home Tree. Nothing. She flew through Pixie Hollow. For a wingbeat, she hovered over a patch of itchy ivy. Then she flew on.

Suddenly, she heard the noise. *Boom!* There was a low rumble in the distance. A flash lit the sky.

Myka had to get closer. She had to see what was happening. She flew toward the noise and lights. The rumblings turned to roars. The flashes grew brighter.

Everything looked strange in the on-again, off-again flare of light. *Boom!*

She saw a gnarled tree bent over, its bare branches sweeping the ground. *Boom!* She spotted a towering beehive. It swayed from the thick trunk of a maple tree.

She swerved around it and kept flying. *Boom!* The spooky light cast long shadows from trees . . . plants . . . rocks.

Everything seemed different. But she was a scout. She had to keep going.

Besides, she was curious about what was going on. The sky was growing brighter now. Spying an open field, Myka settled to the ground.

Round red flowers covered the field. Their petals gathered together at the tips.

Why, she thought, *they look like fluffy balls. I wonder if Lily would know what they are.*

Poof! Each flower let out a puff of tangy air. Myka waved a hand to clear it away from her face. All her senses tingled. Something was about to happen. She forgot about the strange flowers.

A dark shape moved across the sky. Was it a giant black cloud?

Bang! Crash! An ear-splitting roar shook the field. The sky lit up with a dazzling brightness. Lightning! Myka realized. And thunder!

A major storm was brewing. And the way the wind was blowing, it would hit the Home Tree in no time.

Myka took off for Pixie Hollow.

Now she didn't stop to wonder about the sights and sounds. She flew with all her strength.

Home at last! She zipped through her open window. Already she was sounding the alarm. She blew three sharp blasts on a reed whistle by her bed. Danger! Danger! Danger! She flew through the halls, pounding on doors.

"Wake up!" she shouted.

Sleepy fairies poked their heads out of their rooms.

Bess, an art talent, wrapped her smocklike robe around her. "What is it?"

"Thunderstorm!" Myka called over her shoulder. "A big one! Check for weak branches! Latch your windows!"

Other scouts were already moving—

helping and guiding fairies and sparrow men.

"Our rooms are all set!" said Beck. She drew the other animal talents to her side. "Now what should we do?"

"We'll have to wait it out!" Myka prodded a slow-moving Tinker Bell. "Everyone! To the root cellar. We'll be safe there. Come on, come on!"

She herded fairies down through the trunk of the Home Tree. "Hurry! Over here!" She pointed into the dark, windowless space by the roots.

"There," Myka said, finally satisfied. The fairies sat huddled together in row upon row. They were all fully awake. And most looked scared. "The only thing we can do is wait."

So the fairies waited. Time passed, and they waited some more. Some fairies slumped against the bumpy walls and fell asleep again. A few talked quietly.

Myka paced back and forth. She kept one ear cocked, listening. Finally, a rumbling noise made everyone sit up straight.

"Oops!" Tink rubbed her stomach. "Just feeling a little hungry, I guess."

Myka nodded. "We all are," she said. "But we shouldn't go anywhere. The storm will be here any second."

Bess edged closer to Myka. Her face was pale. "You know," she said, "Vidia is still out there."

Vidia, a fast-flying fairy, lived by herself in a sour-plum tree. She liked it

that way. And Myka had to admit, the other fairies did, too. Vidia could be sly—a little nasty, in fact. Still, Vidia shouldn't be out there alone. Not with a dangerous thunderstorm on the way.

The news spread from fairy to sparrow man to fairy. "Vidia is outside!" "Vidia is in trouble!"

Everyone turned to Myka.

"I'll go warn her!" Myka leaped through the door.

"Hooray for Myka!" shouted Tink.

Another scout talent, Trak, followed more slowly behind. "Wait, Myka!" he called. "I'll come, too."

But Myka didn't hear him. She was so determined to find Vidia, she didn't notice Trak—or anything else.

"Vidia!" she cried. "Vidia! There's a thunderstorm! Stay calm! I'm coming!"

Kicking up a puff of dirt, Myka landed by Vidia's sour-plum tree. She looked around, hands on hips. "Well," she said, surprised. "What do you know!"

The sky was a dazzling blue. The sun shone brightly. There was no storm in sight.

And Vidia sat calmly on a branch outside her home.

"Why, what's wrong, Myka?" Vidia asked in her fake-sweet voice. "You didn't think there was any danger, did you?" She shook her head, as if in pity for the poor mistaken scout.

Myka didn't say anything. Of

course she had thought there was danger!

What was going on?

Vidia pointed toward the lagoon. Captain Hook's pirate ship bobbed in the water. "It's just some cannon practice, darling," she said. "They're about ready to fire again."

Boom! Crash! An earsplitting noise filled the air. Sparks flew. Lights flashed as the cannon flared.

It *had* been the pirates—not thunder and lightning. Black smoke rose like a giant storm cloud from the ship.

Vidia was right. There'd been no danger. No danger at all.

Don't miss any of the magical
Disney Fairies chapter books!

course she had thought there was danger!

What was going on?

Vidia pointed toward the lagoon. Captain Hook's pirate ship bobbed in the water. "It's just some cannon practice, darling," she said. "They're about ready to fire again."

Boom! Crash! An earsplitting noise filled the air. Sparks flew. Lights flashed as the cannon flared.

It *had* been the pirates—not thunder and lightning. Black smoke rose like a giant storm cloud from the ship.

Vidia was right. There'd been no danger. No danger at all.

Don't miss any of the magical
Disney Fairies chapter books!

A Masterpiece for Bess

Bess closed the door behind Rosetta. She felt extremely flattered—and still a little stunned. It was part of her role as an art talent to do paintings for her fellow fairies. Till that morning, they had always been for special occasions: an Arrival Day portrait, or a new painting for the Home Tree corridor. In between, she was as free as a bird to paint whatever she wanted.

But now, right out of the blue, *two* fairies wanted their pictures painted in one day! That was a record for any art-talent fairy, Bess was sure.

Bless my wings, she thought. *Who knew that Never fairies had such great taste!*

Tink, North of Never Land

She'd been flying for a quarter of an hour when she looked down. Her heart sank. She was just crossing Havendish Stream.

At this rate, it will take me weeks to reach the Northern Shore! she thought.

But as luck would have it, the wind suddenly shifted in Tink's direction. She felt the carrier bumping against her heels.

Tink climbed into the basket. She let the wind speed her along. In no time, she had reached the edge of Pixie Hollow. Never Land's forest spread out below her like a great dark sea.

Silvermist and the Ladybug Curse

By now, other fairies had gathered around Silvermist. The ladybug sat perfectly still atop the water-talent fairy's head.

"You know," a garden-talent fairy named Rosetta mused, "there's an old superstition about white ladybugs. They're supposed to bring—"

"Bad luck!" Iris said, screeching to a stop in front of Silvermist.

A few fairies chuckled uncertainly. No one took Iris very seriously. But fairies were superstitious creatures. They believed in wishes, charms, and luck—both good and bad.

"The white ladybug!" Iris's voice rose higher and higher. "It's cursed!"